1. On his way to the Mr Men New Year's party, Mr Bump had one of his little accidents. He fell over in the snow.

2. Oops! Mr Bump started to roll down a hill. Over and over he tumbled. Soon he caught up with his Mr Men friends.

3. Bump! First he rolled into Mr Slow. Then. Bump. Bump. Bump. Into the other Mr Men. What an enormous snowball!

4. Mr Chatterbox had arrived earlier. 'Well,' he said. 'That's one way of getting to a party. HAPPY NEW YEAR!'

1. Mr Forgetful was a little forgetful. You can say that again. Mr Forgetful was a little forgetful. One morning in Forget-me-not Cottage, which was where he lived, the telephone rang. It was Mr Happy.

2. 'Just thought I'd remind you. We're meeting for lunch today. One o'clock at Lucky's', he said. Mr Forgetful was silent. 'You've forgotten, haven't you?' laughed Mr Happy. Mr Forgetful thought. 'Forgotten what?'

3. Mr Forgetful set off for town. 'Lucky's at one. Lucky's at one,' he said over and over to himself. On the way he met Mr Nosey. 'Where are you off to?' Mr Nosey asked. 'The Sticky Bun,' replied Mr Forgetful.

4. When he reached town, Mr Forgetful went to the restaurant. The wrong one! By the time he remembered which was the right one, he was nearly an hour late. Mr Happy was waiting outside. 'I'm glad you didn't forget,' he smiled.

5. The two friends were shown to a table, and looked at the menu. The waitress came up to take their orders. 'What will you have to start?' she asked. Mr Forgetful looked puzzled. 'Start what?' he said.

6. They both decided on soup, but when the waitress brought it Mr Forgetful couldn't remember whether he'd asked for chicken or oxtail. But they sorted that out, and enjoyed the rest of the meal, and soon it was time to go.

7. Mr Forgetful spent a long time trying to remember where he had put his hat. And some more time trying to remember which hat was his. But finally he found the right one, and he and Mr Happy said goodbye, and left.

8. 'I think I'd better see you home,' laughed Mr Happy. 'You've probably forgotten the way!' As they walked along, chatting happily, a small figure in the distance called, 'Sir, sir. You've forgotten to pay the bill.'

LITTLE MISS HELPFUL ON THE FARM

Little Miss Helpful wasn't really.

What?

Helpful.

She was one of those people who loved helping but ended up making matters worse.

Like the time she helped Mr Clumsy to tie his untidy shoelaces.

Somehow, little Miss Helpful managed to tie Mr Clumsy's shoelaces together, so that he fell over, headfirst into a flowerbed!

Or, like the time last summer, when little Miss Helpful went to buy some eggs from Farmer Fields.

'Sorry,' said Farmer Fields, 'I haven't any eggs to sell today. My wife is in bed with a bad cold and I haven't had time to collect them.'

'Let me help!' cried little Miss Helpful. And, before Farmer Fields could stop her, she was racing round the farmyard looking for eggs.

First, she went to the cowshed.

'Moo!' said a cow who had just been milked.

'Ooo!' screamed little Miss Helpful and jumped backwards into a bucket of milk.

Somehow the bucket got stuck on her foot and went Clang! Clang! Clang! on the cowshed floor.

Which.

Frightened all the cows so that they ran out into the farmyard, mooing.

'Come back!' shouted little Miss Helpful, who came out of the cowshed with the bucket on her foot.

Clang! Clang! Clang!

That woke the farm dog sleeping in his kennel so that he began to bark.

Which.

Disturbed the rooster sitting on the roof of the kennel, so that he began to crow, 'Cock-a-doodle-doo!' at the top of his voice.

All of which woke the farmer's wife, who had been asleep in bed with her cold. She came downstairs to see what was the matter.

Just then, little Miss Helpful gave a shout.

'Eggs!' she cried. 'Dozens of them!'

Where do you think?

In the hen house of course!

'Now, why didn't I think of looking there?' she said. And little Miss Helpful popped the eggs into a basket, one by one.

Then she hurried over to the farmhouse. The bucket was still stuck on her foot. Clang! Clang! Clang!

And somehow, little Miss Helpful just bumped into Farmer Fields, who was rushing across the farmyard to rescue his cows, and . . . dropped all the eggs.

'Oh no!' wailed the farmer's wife, 'whatever shall we do?'

'Don't worry,' said little Miss Helpful.

'I'll help!'

GREEDY GRUB

What will Mr Greedy choose for his meal? Everything! Look at the plates on the table and pair the food into five familiar things to eat. Then write your answers on the menu.

MENU

. . . . . . and . . . . . .

. . . . . . and . . . . . .

. . . . . . and . . . . . .

. . . . . . and . . . . . .

. . . . . . and . . . . . .

Poor Mr Worry. He does worry. About the weather especially! Hidden in this puzzle are twenty words about the weather. See if you can find them all. They read across, or down, or diagonally.

BREEZE
CLOUD
DRIZZLE
FLOOD
FOG
FROST
GALE
HAIL
HEATWAVE
ICE
LIGHTNING
MIST
RAIN
SHOWER
SLEET
SNOW
STORM
SUNSHINE
THUNDER
WIND

```
          S N O W
        X U M I S T A
    F O G G N D F C L O U D
  F L G R U S V R L R I E T
  M O S I E H F O I O C C H
  O P R A I N S G Z E Z U
  D N G U N R T H S Z S N U
U B B R E E Z E T T M L D N
H E A T W A V E N O J E E A
C L O O M D J G I R K E R V
A H H A I L Q E N M M T T I
S V W I N D W G A L E Y
```

Colour in all the parts with a dot in them to find two objects that are very useful when Mr Nosey is around.

Here is a rhyme about Mr Nosey. Can you complete the last line by putting the mixed up words in the right order?

Mr Nosey saw a keyhole,
And through it he did spy.
But someone put a key in it,
And . . . . !

black was the one eye result

Answer: And the result was one black eye!

17

MR. MUDDLE'S STORYTIME PUZZLE

These pictures tell a story, but Mr Muddle has muddled them. Can you number the pictures to put them in the right order?

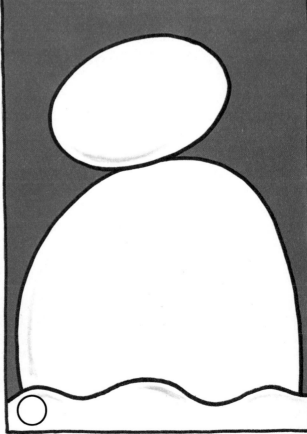

MR. SMALL
THE GREAT INVENTOR

One morning, Mr Small woke up in his tiny bed, in his tiny house, which, by the way, is under a daisy at the bottom of Mr Robinson's garden.

'I wish I could do something useful,' he thought, 'but there aren't many little jobs a little person like me can do.'

Then he began to think about some of the little jobs he had tried to do, with not very much success.

For example, he had tried working in the post office.

Sticking stamps on to parcels.

But he kept getting stuck to the stamps. And he was posted through the letterbox three times in one week. By mistake. So, of course, he had to leave that job.

Once he got a job in a flower shop.

Watering the flowers.

Nothing difficult about that, you might think. But he kept falling into the watering can! So he didn't last long in that job.

Then, only last week, Mr Robinson found him a job in a sport shop.

Polishing ping-pong balls!

But Mr Small kept slipping off the balls into the box. So he had to leave that job, too.

Now, on this particular morning, Mr Small got out of bed and went downstairs to breakfast and had another think about the sort of job he could do.

It wasn't easy.

At first.

Then it came to him.

'If only I could invent something,' he thought, as he sipped a drop of tea.

'I could be an INVENTOR!' he cried, as he sliced a crumb of toast.

But could he think of anything to invent?

No, he could not!

So after breakfast, Mr Small decided to go and see his friend Mr Robinson and ask his advice.

It took him all morning to walk up the garden path.

After all, he's only little!

Mr Robinson was sitting in his garden, in a deck chair, reading a book.

'Hello,' said Mr Robinson. 'What

are you doing today?'

'Nothing much,' replied Mr Small.

And then he told Mr Robinson about his idea. 'I want to be an inventor,' he said. 'But I can't think of anything to invent and I'm not sure where to begin.'

'Hmm,' pondered Mr Robinson. 'I have a friend who may be able to help you. Come along. I'll take you to see him straightaway.'

Mr Robinson put Mr Small in his car and drove into town. He stopped the car outside a big, important looking building. Carrying Mr Small, he went up to the front door and rang the bell.

The door was opened by a man wearing a long, white coat.

'This is Professor Knowitall,' said Mr Robinson.

'Come in, come in,' said Professor Knowitall, who was, by the way, a professor of science and an inventor at the New Brainwave University.

'I'd like to invent something!' said Mr Small.

'Good, good,' said the professor. 'You can work in my laboratory and see how you get on.'

Mr Small stayed for a week.

On Monday, he invented a fully automatic, computerised knitting machine, for knitting socks.

One hundred and one socks a minute.

'One hundred and one?' Mr Small asked himself. 'That's odd.'

'Odd socks, I'm afraid,' smiled Professor Knowitall.

So he didn't get far with that invention.

On Tuesday, Mr Small invented the recipe for a revolutionary new jam doughnut.

I expect you'd like to know more about that, wouldn't you?

Sorry. Can't tell you.

It's a secret!

Unfortunately, Mr Greedy popped in to see how Mr Small was getting on.

'Just testing,' he said, licking his fingers.

'I think you mean, just TASTING!' said Mr Small as he watched Mr Greedy pop the last revolutionary new jam doughnut into his mouth.

So he didn't get very far with that invention.

But, by the end of the week, Mr Small had made a technological breakthrough. He had invented something that was to make him the man he is today.

He invented the world's smallest electronic component ever. The micro-PIP!

Half the size of a micro-chip, at least.

If not smaller.

Brilliant!

Professor Knowitall was delighted.

'You should write about your great invention,' said the professor. 'Famous inventors always do.'

'All right,' said Mr Small, 'I will.'

And he did.

It was only a short story. After all, he is only little.

And guess what?

You've just read it!

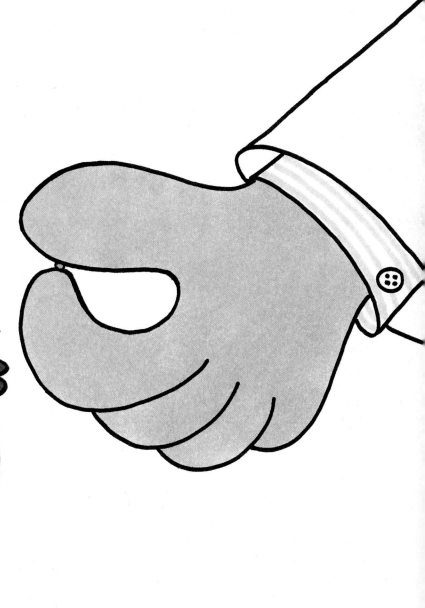

How to make a wobbly Mr. Funny Invitation Card

The easiest way is to make some photocopies of page 27, which you can then colour with crayons or water-based felt tips. Or if you prefer, you can trace on to stiff white paper. Cut out the three pieces. Fold the largest one in half which then makes the inside of your card. Paste the front on the front of the card (be careful here because it is all too easy to paste it on the back by mistake and then you would feel very silly!) Fold the strip which comes off the top of Mr Funny's hat down behind him, and attach it to the right-hand page of your card with a *spot* of paste in the place shown, making sure that his hand does not cross over the centre fold of the card.

LET THE PASTE DRY!

Now you can stand the card up, and watch Mr Funny wobble in the breeze.

glue

fold

Come to a Party

on ....

at ....

....

....

Time ....

to ....

from

....

and
Mr. Funny

glue

Mr. Bump.

string

eye hole

eye hole

string

Trace the Mr Men on to some stout white drawing paper, and colour them with your felt tips or crayons.

Then cut them out round the white outline, cut out the eye holes, and tie strings long enough to go round your head, at the sides, in the positions shown.

28

You could try making other Mr Men into masks as well, but remember to keep the positions of the eye and string holes the same.

MR. CLEVER'S MR. MEN QUIZ

How well do you know the Mr Men? Answer these questions correctly, and you're a real Mr Men mastermind. You can check your answers at the bottom of the page.

1. Who is small and round, and has extraordinary long arms?
2. What is the name of the amazing Mr Man who can make himself invisible?
3. Which Mr Man filled Mr Funny's hat with treacle?
4. Whose snore sounds like a herd of elephants?
5. In which Mr Man story are there red-nosed dogs chasing red-nosed cats chasing red-nosed mice?
6. Who made everybody extremely cross by putting all the books upside down on the library shelves?
7. Which Mr Man went to stay with Mr Greedy to try to increase his appetite?
8. Who had to leave his job in a sweet shop because he kept falling into the sweet jars?
9. What is the name of Mr Slow's next door neighbour?
10. Which Mr Man lives in Loudland?

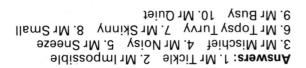

Answers: 1. Mr Tickle 2. Mr Impossible 3. Mr Mischief 4. Mr Noisy 5. Mr Sneeze 6. Mr Topsy Turvy 7. Mr Skinny 8. Mr Small 9. Mr Busy 10. Mr Quiet

30

Oh calamity! Oh disaster!
What ferocious animal
has given Mr Jelly such
a fright? Join the
dots and find out.

MR.FUNNY WINS A CUP

1. Mr Funny was having lunch. Fish finger soup! He was enjoying a second cup of soup when there was a knock at the door of his funny teapot house. He went to see who it was.

2. There, on the doorstep, was little Miss Dotty. 'Hello,' said Mr Funny. 'You look lost.' Miss Dotty sighed. 'I am,' she said. 'I can't find my way home to Nonsenseland, and I want to be back for the Nonsense Cup competition.'

3. As you may know, every year in Nonsenseland the King awards a Cup to the person with the silliest idea of the year. 'Don't worry,' smiled Mr Funny, 'I'll take you home in my car.' Mr Funny's car is a shoe!

4. As Mr Funny and Miss Dotty drove along in Mr Funny's shoe, everybody laughed at such a funny sight. Even the flowers giggled to themselves. Then Mr Funny noticed the grass was blue. They were in Nonsenseland.

5. Mr Funny drove into the City Square just as Mr Nonsense was showing his silly idea to the crowd. It was an umbrella. Full of holes. 'To water the plants when it rains,' he explained. The crowd clapped.

6. Then it was Mr Silly's turn. He had invented an elasticated dog lead for lazy people who didn't like walking the dog! Isn't that silly? The crowd cheered, and Mr Silly felt sure he would win the Cup.

7. The King stood up. 'Ladies and gentlemen,' he said to the crowd. 'We have seen some very silly ideas today, and so it is my pleasure to . . .' And then he stopped. He was looking at Mr Funny's car in amazement.

8. 'Whose car is that?' cried the King. 'Why, it's a shoe. How silly!' Little Miss Dotty called out, 'It's Mr Funny's car,' and Mr Funny blushed. 'That,' said the King, 'is quite the silliest idea ever! Mr Funny has won the Cup!'

Have fun making this model of Mr. Lazy!

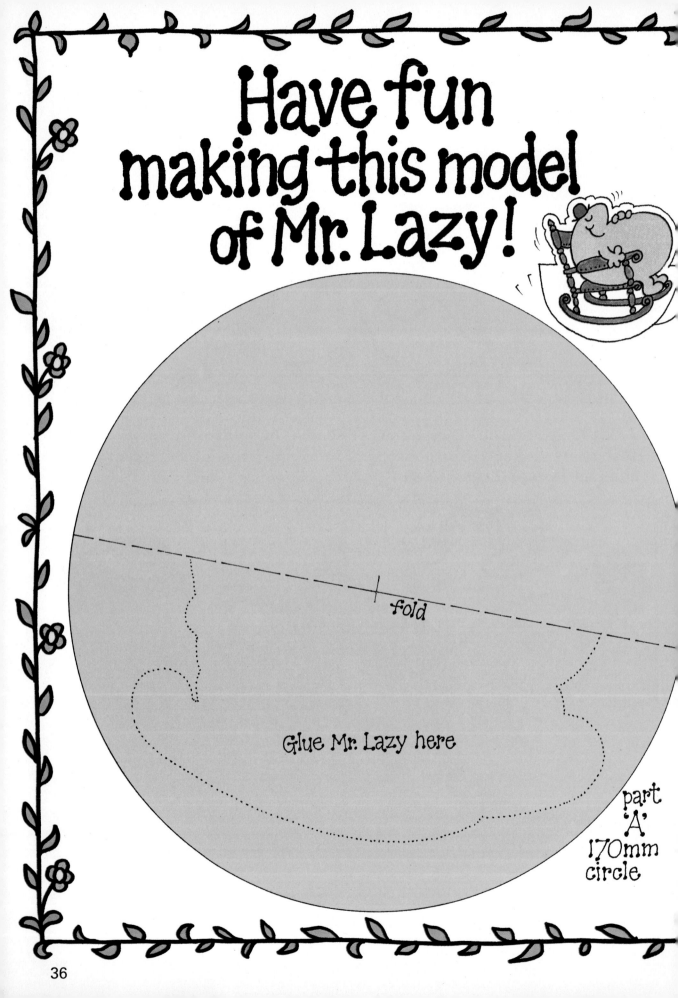

fold

Glue Mr. Lazy here

part 'A' 170mm circle

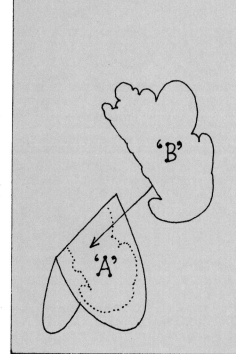

Have fun making this paper model of Mr Lazy in his rocking chair.

Trace the circle and the figure of Mr Lazy on to a piece of stout white paper or thin card.

Cut out the two parts 'A' and 'B', and colour them with your crayons or felt tips.

Fold the circle across the middle and glue Mr Lazy in the position shown.

Give him a rock, and just watch him sleep! You can almost hear him snoring!

part 'B'
cut out
round
this line

ON THE BEACH

Have fun colouring this seaside picture. How many flags can you see? How many sandcastles are there? How many Mr Men are eating ice cream?

THERE
ARE . . . ☐ flags

☐ sandcastles

☐ ice creams

39

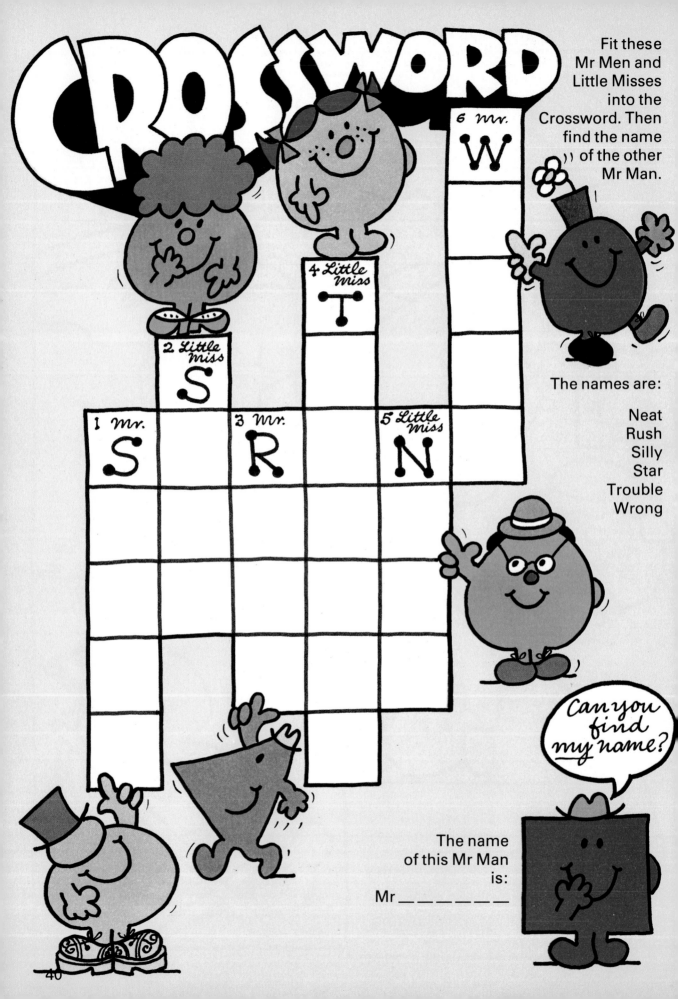

CROSSWORD

Fit these Mr Men and Little Misses into the Crossword. Then find the name of the other Mr Man.

The names are:

Neat
Rush
Silly
Star
Trouble
Wrong

Can you find my name?

The name of this Mr Man is:

Mr _ _ _ _ _ _ _

40

Trace off the two parts of the bookmark and transfer to stout paper. Colour Mr Small using felt tips or crayons. Then cut out the two parts carefully.

Fold in the side flaps of the slide and thread, arrow end first, down through cut A and out again through cut B.

Make sure you have Mr Small's arm and hat showing on the front, then unfold the two side flaps, which stop the slide from coming right out of the bookmark.

Now fold over the back of the bookmark and paste down.

Work the tab up and down, and Mr Small will raise his hat to you.

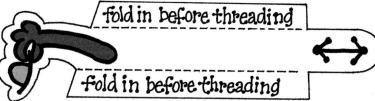

fold in before threading

fold in before threading

Book Mark

fold → ← fold

))

cut A

Always be polite like Mr. Small!

cut B

✪✪✪ MR. STRONG'S

Mr Strong wants you to help him sort these eggs. Can you count how many brown eggs, white eggs, and speckled eggs there are? Write your answers on the corresponding hen baskets at the bottom of the page.

BROWN

WHITE

SPECKLED

EGGSTRAORDINARY PUZZLES

Which two eggs are exactly alike?

Mr Strong has dropped his eggs. Can you match the broken pieces together to make four whole eggs?

43

AT THE BUS STOP

A story without words

What a sneeze! Little Miss Scatterbrain's hat has landed on top of Mr Funny's head. But where has his gone? Who is wearing little Miss Bossy's hat? And what has happened to Mr Small's?

Mr Rush was in too much of a hurry to finish these portraits. Can you complete them for him? When you have, why not colour them with your felt tipped pens or crayons.

MR. DIZZY

LITTLE MISS TINY

LITTLE MISS CHATTERBOX

MR. SNEEZE

MR. TALL

MR. FUSSY

MR. IMPOSSIBLE

MR. BUMP BUYS A CAR

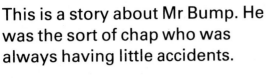

This is a story about Mr Bump. He was the sort of chap who was always having little accidents.

If there was something to bump into or trip over or smash, you may be sure Mr Bump would be there, bumping, tripping and smashing. Poor chap. It happened all the time.

One day, Mr Bump decided to buy a car. He was fed up with walking everywhere. Tripping over pavements and bumping into lamp posts.

He went along to the car showroom and talked to the salesman.

'I'd like to buy a car,' said Mr Bump.

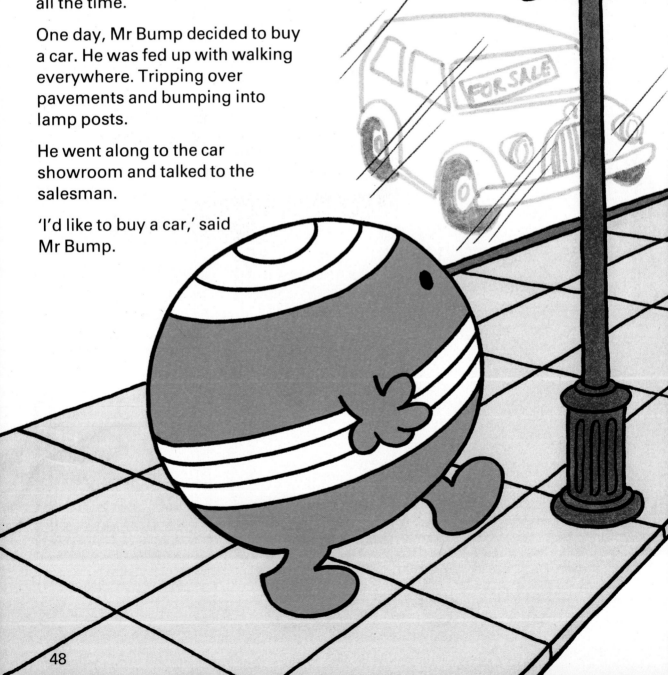

'Certainly,' said the salesman. 'I have the very one for you, Mr Bump. Extra large bumpers!' he said, knowingly.

Mr Bump's car was new and shiny.

'I think I'll drive to the seaside,' said Mr Bump, getting in and slamming the door.

'Ouch!' he cried, sucking his bruised fingers which had accidentally got shut in the door.

Mr Bump started the engine.

'Which way to the seaside?' he asked.

'That way,' said the salesman.

'Thank you,' said Mr Bump, reversing into all the new cars in the showroom.

CRASH!

'Sorry!' said Mr Bump.

'So am I,' said the salesman, looking at all the ruined cars.

Mr Bump drove off down the High Street. He saw a postman delivering letters.

'Which way to the seaside?' asked Mr Bump.

'First left,' replied the postman.

'Thank you,' said Mr Bump, turning straight into somebody's front garden. He drove through the fence and over the flowerbed.

SMASH!

'Sorry,' said Mr Bump.

'So am I,' said the owner of the flowerbed, who just happened to be Mr Fussy. You could say that Mr Fussy was furious about his fence and his flowers!

Mr Bump drove slowly out of the flowerbed, down the road and round a corner . . . straight into the back of a big, red bus.

BUMP!

They were bumper to bumper!

'Sorry!' said Mr Bump.

'So am I,' said the bus driver and he got down from his bus to inspect the damage. One small dent in the bus. One very large dent in Mr Bump's new car.

'Where were you going?' asked the driver.

'I was going to the seaside,' said Mr Bump, looking sadly at his car.

'Well,' smiled the bus driver, 'that's just where I'm going. This bus will take you all the way.'

So Mr Bump went to the seaside after all. He sat on top of the bus and enjoyed the view. Not a bump in sight!

And do you know what?

When Mr Bump got to the seaside, he found a car that suited him down to the ground. The sort of car that he could bump around in as much as he liked.

Can you guess what sort of car that was? That's right.

A bumper car! At the fairground.

BUMP! There he goes again!

MAGIC

change Mr Noisy into Mr Quiet!

Show your friends a square of paper with a picture of Mr Noisy glued in the middle.

Fold in the sides of the square to the middle, hiding the picture.

mr Noisy.

Take the folded square between the palms of your hands, rubbing it gently, and muttering the magic words . . . 'Go away Mr Noisy . . . come in Mr Quiet!'

Then lay the paper flat on the table again, open up the folds and, lo and behold, Mr Noisy has gone and there in his place is Mr Quiet! Marvellous! Take a bow!

mr Quiet.

TRICKS!

The Disappearing Counter

Show your audience a sheet of paper upon which is a coin, a glass tumbler standing upside down, and a handkerchief.

Open the handkerchief and spread it over the tumbler so that the tumbler is completely hidden.

Moving handkerchief and tumbler together over the coin, wave your hand or wand. Then remove the handkerchief with a flourish. 'Hey presto!' The coin has completely disappeared.

Replace the handkerchief over the tumbler, and move them together to one side. 'Hey presto!' the coin reappears.

Turn the page to find out how these tricks are done . . .

How to change Mr. Noisy into Mr. Quiet!

You actually have *two* identical squares of paper. One has a picture of Mr Noisy glued in the middle and the other a picture of Mr Quiet.

You can trace all this from page 52.

Fold *both* pieces *exactly* the same way. Then glue their middles back to back, taking care that they fit properly so that the extra folds do not show.

Then, when you are performing the trick, all you have to remember, as you rub the folded paper between your hands, it to put it down on the table the other way up, just before you unfold it.

Practise in front of a mirror before you try the trick on your friends.

TOP SECRET Don't tell anyone—EVER!

How you make the counter disappear!

Use a piece of the same paper that you are going to put on the table, and cut out a disc to fit over the mouth of the tumbler. Carefully glue it on the rim, and trim it very carefully so that the edges do not show.

Then as long as you remember to keep the tumbler upside down, and only slide it about on the paper, no one will guess that its mouth is covered.

Have fun! Practise this one in front of a mirror too!

MR. HAPPY'S JOKE PAGE

Mr Happy: I bet I can make you speak like a Red Indian.
How?
Mr Happy: Told you so!

Miss Bossy: No more food before bed, Mr Greedy. You must not sleep on a full tummy.
Mr Greedy: Don't worry! I always sleep on my back!

Mr Dizzy: I don't understand. Mr Clever says there's no such thing as a whole day.
Mr Happy: He's right, Mr Dizzy. Because day always BREAKS and night FALLS!

Knock, knock.
Who's there?
You.
You who?
Did you call?

'Quick, quack. Quick, quack.'
What was that? Mr Silly's impression of a duck in a hurry.

MR. MISCHIEF'S NEW YEAR

One New Year's Eve, Mr Mischief was sitting at home making a list of New Year's resolutions. Not good ones. Oh no. Not Mr Mischief. He was making a list of all the naughty things he was going to do in the New Year.

He was still writing when his clock struck midnight. And that gave Mr Mischief the idea for his naughtiest trick yet.

Mr Mischief got up, went to a cupboard and found a small box.

Then he took the box and ran out of the house as fast as his little legs would carry him.

He ran all the way into town, giggling as he ran. He couldn't wait to try out his latest piece of mischief.

When Mr Mischief reached the town, he went straight to the Town Hall and looked up at the clock. Then, when he was quite sure no one was looking, he went to a little door at the side of the Town Hall and opened it.

Inside was a staircase that led all the way up to the Town Hall clock. Mr Mischief ran up the stairs faster than his little legs could carry him. Which is very fast, I can tell you.

At the top of the stairs, Mr Mischief stopped and listened.

Tick, tock. Tick, tock.

The Town Hall clock was ticking away as it had always done. Day in. Day out. It was the best clock for miles around and everyone depended on it.

Mr Mischief listened again.

Tick, tock. Tick, tock.

Then, he crept right up to the clock, and opened the box. Can you guess what he was going to put inside?

Tick, tock. Tick, tock.

Mr Mischief reached out and took the tick, tock right out of the clock and popped it into his box.

And, of course, you know what happened to the clock, don't you? It stopped. Not a tick or a tock to be heard.

'Got you!' giggled Mr Mischief as he ran down the stairs. 'Ooo, what glorious mischief,' he chuckled as he skipped outside. 'First trick of the year!'

Just at that moment, Mr Happy came round the corner. He was on his way home from a party.

'Happy New Year!' said Mr Happy. 'What have you got in that box?'

Mr Mischief tried to hide it behind his back. 'Er . . . it's just a little New Year's Eve surprise,' he said and ran off home.

'Hm?' thought Mr Happy. 'I wonder what Mr Mischief has been up to?'

The next morning, there was chaos!

Everyone was late because the clock had stopped.

The milkman was late delivering Mr Happy's milk.

The news reader on the radio was late reading the news. He read the seven o'clock news at half-past ten!

The policeman on traffic duty was late. The town was full of angry drivers all stuck in traffic jams.

And Mr Greedy's favourite restaurant was late opening. The waiter served breakfast when he should have been serving lunch and lunch when he should have been serving tea!

Everyone was very cross.

Mr Clever went along to the Town Hall to have a look at the clock, to see if he could mend it. After all, Mr Clever is the Cleverest Person in the World.

'What is the matter with it?' asked Mr Happy.

'Er . . .' began Mr Clever. 'I'm afraid I don't know.'

'Well, that's not very clever of you, is it?' said Mr Happy. Then he thought for a moment and said, 'But there is someone who might know. Someone I remember who was here last night with a little New Year's Eve surprise in a box . . .'

Later that day, Mr Happy went to call on Mr Mischief. He took a friend with him. Little Miss Magic!

Mr Mischief opened the door. 'Hello,' he said. 'What do you want?'

'Nothing much,' smiled Mr Happy. 'Just a little of your . . . time.'

'It won't take more than a tick,' smiled little Miss Magic, quickly stepping inside and spotting the box.

'A tick and a tock at the very most,' grinned Mr Happy, winking at little Miss Magic.

Then little Miss Magic pointed to the box and said, 'OPEN!'

And it did.

Then little Miss Magic told the tick, tock to start ticking.

And it did.

Tick, tock. Tick, tock.

'LOUDER!' ordered little Miss Magic.

And it did. Tick, tock! TICK, TOCK! Louder and louder until Mr Mischief begged it to stop.

'Promise there will be no more naughty tricks?' said little Miss Magic, sternly.

'What! No more tricks!' cried Mr Mischief.

'Promise, or else,' said little Miss Magic drumming her fingers on the box.

'Oh, all right,' said Mr Mischief.

Then little Miss Magic commanded the ticking to stop and closed the box.

TICK·TOCK·TICK·TOCK·TICK·TOCK·**TICK·TOCK**

'Time to go,' said Mr Happy. 'We must put the tick, tock back into the Town Hall clock.'

'No sooner said than DONE!' smiled little Miss Magic and she opened the box to let the tick, tock fly back to the Town Hall.

'That's amazing!' laughed Mr Happy.

'I know,' smiled little Miss Magic. 'I suppose you could say, it's amazing how . . . time flies!'

61

AMAZING RACE

Miss a throw!

'B'

Have another throw!

Turn right → next throw

Go to 'A'

Mr. Strong

Mr. Noisy

Mr. Small

Mr. Bump

Throw a six to start

Turn here next go ↓

Trace off the Mr Men counters and paste them on to 2p pieces. Colour them with felt tips or crayons.
You will need a dice and shaker to play. Throw a six to start, and then follow any way you like through the garden maze, just obeying the instructions on the squares you land on.
First one home is the winner. Have fun!

'A'

Throw a six to go on!